I0550226

*The Sayings
of
Thomas Carlyle*

Thomas Carlyle

The Sayings

of

Thomas Carlyle

Selected and with an introduction

by Brendan King

D.O.R. Books

ISBN: 978-1-870835-03-9
Introduction and editorial arrangement © 1993
Brendan King

INTRODUCTION

Since his death in 1881, Thomas Carlyle's reputation as a writer, and his influence as an historian, have both steadily declined. By his own reckoning, this would be a conclusive proof of the incorrectness of his ideas, for, as he himself remarked, "give a thing a hundred years, and if it is still believed it be right." Time has, however, not just shown that some of his views are wrong, but that, indeed, to many they are deeply offensive. Carlyle's work has suffered more than that of many of his contemporaries by being seen through the moralistic eyes of the present day. His belief, as expressed in *On Heroes, Hero Worship and the Heroic in History*, that great men should be trusted with absolute power, has not found favour in an era scarred by totalitarianism and political oppression, the inevitable consequences of allowing such power to fall into the hands of men like Hitler and Stalin.

Yet Carlyle's present unpopularity is not simply due to the disagreeableness of some of his ideas, nor is it entirely due to the difficulty of his style or the length of some of his major works (it was said that Gertrude Stein was the last person known to have read every line of *Frederick the Great*), but has as much do to with the fact that his work as a whole does not present a consistent philosophy. It has been impossible to classify him either as a thinker on the Left or the Right of the political spectrum, and as a result he has never really been adopted or championed by either side. Like many a Scot, Carlyle said what he meant and damn the consequences, and so, rather uncomfortably, one can find oneself agreeing passionately with him one moment, and being outraged by his bigotry the next.

Many of the issues that concerned him most are still with us today — the inequalities between the rich and the poor, notions of freedom and democracy, and questions of individual responsibility. A collection of Carlyle's sayings is, of course, no substitute for actually reading his work, nor can it paint as comprehensive and rounded a portrait as that which James Anthony Froude gives us in his definitive Life, but it does give a hint of the power that Carlyle had in his command over language, a power that raised him to undreamed of, if not necessarily long-lived, heights of prestige and influence over virtually all of his literary contemporaries.

Abbreviations

CL = *Collected Letters of Thomas and Jane Welsh Carlyle*, Duke University Press, 1970-; Col = *Collected Works* (Chapman & Hall, 1869-71) 30 vols; K = *The Early Kings of Norway: Also an Essay on the Portraits of John Knox*, Chapman & Hall, 1875; JAF = *Thomas Carlyle: A History of the First Forty Years of His Life 1795-1835* and *A History of His Life in London 1834-1881* by J. A. Froude (Longmans Green, 1882-1884) 4 vols; R = *Reminiscences* (Longmans 1882) 2 vols; S = *Thomas Carlyle* by Julian Symons (Gollancz 1952); W = *Life of Thomas Carlyle* by David Wilsonin (Kegan Paul 1923-34) 6 vols; Y = *Carlyle: His Rise and Fall* by Norwood Young (Duckworth 1927).

ON HIS CONTEMPORARIES

Charles Lamb I sincerely believe to be in some considerable degree insane. A more pitiful, rickety, gasping, staggering, stammering Tomfool I do not know. He is witty by denying truisms and abjuring good manners. His speech wiggles hither and thither with an incessant painful fluctuation, not an opinion in it, or a fact, or a phrase that you can thank him for — more like a convulsion fit than a natural systole and diastole. Besides, he is now a confirmed, shameless drunkard; asks vehemently for gin and water in strangers' houses, tipples till he is utterly mad, and is only not thrown out of doors because he is too much despised for taking such trouble with him. Poor Lamb! Poor England, when such a despicable abortion is named genius! *JAF 2.209*

Kemble was there, a most jerking disturbed, violent-vapid, brown-gypsy piece of Selfconceit and Greenroomism. [John Kemble] *JAF 3.155*

Sir David Innes, if, indeed, he be a knight of flesh and blood, and not a mere shadowy personification of dullness, snored assiduously beside me all night, and talked the most polite ineptitudes all day. *JAF 1.217*

This night Gordon invites me to meet him at supper, but I cannot resolve to go; the man is not worth an indigestion. [John Gordon] *JAF 2.343*

There is only one post fit for you, and that is the office of perpetual president of the Heaven and Hell Amalgamation Society. [Lord Houghton. *Attr.*]

Two or three squires of the neighbourhood have looked in upon us of late, but their minds are what Pump Sandy calls a "vaaccum". *JAF 1.207*

There goes [Dean] Stanley, boring holes in the bottom of the Church of England! *JAF 4.263*

An immeasurable ass. [Herbert Spencer] *S 241*

I have also seen Thomas Campbell. Him I like worst of all. He is heartless as a little Edinburgh advocate. There is a smirk on his face which would befit a shopman or an auctioneer. His very eye has the cold vivacity of a conceited worldling. His talk is small, contemptuous, and shallow. *JAF 1.220*

His wife has black eyes, a fair skin, a symmetrical but vulgar face; and she speaks with that accursed Celtic accent — a twang which I never yet heard associated with any manly or profitable thought or sentiment, which to me is but the symbol of Highland vanity and filth and famine. [Thomas Campbell's wife] *JAF 1.221*

He is one of those persons whose understanding is overburthened by their memory. [Professor Jameson] *S 47*

A wretched dud called Swinfen Jervis, member I think for Chester, called one day with his wife, a dirty little atheistical radical, living seemingly in a mere element of pretentious twaddle with Sheridan Knowles and James Simpsons, and the literary vapidities of his day. *JAF 3.186*

Poor Shelley always was, and is, a kind of ghastly

object, colourless, pallid, without health or warmth or vigour; the sound of him shrieky, frosty, as if a ghost were trying to "sing to us"; the temperament of him spasmodic, hysterical, instead of strong or robust; with fine affections and aspirations, gone all such a road:— a man infinitely too weak for that solitary scaling of the Alps which he undertook in spite of all the world. [Percy Bysshe Shelley] *R 325*

One of the powerfullest smokers I have ever worked along with. [Lord Tennyson.] *S 166*

The greatest genius that has lived for a century, and the greatest ass that has lived for three. [Johann Wolfgang Goethe] *S 79*

Coleridge is a mass of richest spices putrefied into a dunghill. *JAF 1.293*

I have seen many curiosities; not the least of them I reckon Coleridge, the Kantian metaphysician and quondam Lake poet... Figure a fat, flabby, incurvated personage, at once short, rotund, and relaxed, with a watery mouth, a snuffy nose, a pair of strange brown, timid, yet earnest-looking eyes, a high tapering brow, and a great bush of grey hair; and you have some faint idea of Coleridge. He is a kind good soul, full of religion and affection and poetry and animal magnetism. His cardinal sin is that he wants will. He has no resolution. He shrinks from pain or labour in any of its shapes. His very attitude bespeaks this. He never straightens his knee-joints. He stoops with his fat, ill-shapen shoulders, and in walking he does not tread, but shovel and slide. My father would call it "skluiffing". He is also busied to keep, by strong and frequent inhalations, the water of his mouth from overflowing, and his eyes have a look of anxious impotence. He would do with all his heart, but he knows he dares not. The conversation of the man is much as I anticipated — a forest of thoughts, some true, many false, more part dubious, all of them ingenious in some degree, often in a high degree. But there is no method in his talk; he wanders like a man sailing among many currents, whithersoever his lazy mind directs him; and, what is more unpleasant, he preaches, or rather soliloquizes. He cannot speak, he can only tal—k (so he names it). Hence I found him unprofitable, even tedious; but we parted very good friends, I promising to go back and see him some evening — a promise I fully intend to keep. I sent him a copy of *Meister*, about which we had some friendly talk. I reckon him a man of great and useless genius; a strange, not at all a great man. *JAF 1.222*

Coleridge is sunk inextricably in the depths of putrescent indolence. *JAF 1.263*

Coleridge is a steam-engine of a hundred horses power — with the boiler burst. His talk is resplendent with imagery and the shows of thought; you listen as to an oracle, and find yourself no jot the wiser. He is without beginning or middle or end. A round fat oily yet impatient little man, his mind seems totally beyond his own control; he speaks incessantly, not thinking or imagining or remembering, but combining all these processes into one; as a rich and lazy housewife might mingle her soup and fish and beef and custard into one unspeakable mass and present it trueheartedly to her astonished guests. *CL 3.140* [To Thomas Murray]

May fail to accomplish much. [Lord Macaulay] *JAF 2.373*

At bottom this Macaulay is but a poor creature with his dictionary literature and erudition, his saloon arrogance. He will neither see nor do any great thing, but be a poor Holland House unbeliever, with spectacles instead of eyes, to the end of him. *JAF 3.192*

He carries a laudanum bottle in his pocket, and the venom of a wasp in his heart. [Thomas de Quincey] *JAF 1.263*

One of the prettiest Talkers I ever heard; of great, indeed of diseased *acuteness*, not without depth, of a fine sense too, but of no breadth, no justness; weak, diffuse, supersensitive; on the whole, a perverted, ineffectual man. [Thomas de Quincey] *CL 6.370* [To John Stuart Mill]

Old Rogers stayed the longest, indeed as long as ourselves. I do not remember any old man (he is now eighty-three) whose manner of living gave me less satisfaction. A most sorrowful, distressing, distracted old phenomenon, hovering over the rim of deep eternities with nothing but light babble, fatuity, vanity, and the frostiest London wit in his mouth. Sometimes

I felt as if I could throttle him, the poor wretch! [Samuel Rogers] *JAF 3.403*

An elegant, politely malignant old lady. [Samuel Rogers] *JAF 2.231*

He is a wondrous man to see editing, that Cochrane; what one might call an Editing Pig. [John Dundas Cochrane] *JAF 2.310*

Hunt's household in Cheyne Row, Chelsea. Nondescript! unutterable! [Leigh Hunt] *JAF 2.426*

It is next to an impossibility that a London-born man should not be a stunted one. Most of them, as Hunt, are dwarfed and dislocated into the merest imbeciles. [Leigh Hunt] *JAF 3.25*

No genuine productive Thought was ever revealed by him to mankind; indeed no clear undistorted vision into anything, or picture of anything; but all had a certain falsehood, a brawling theatrical insincere character. The man's moral nature too was bad, his demeanour, as a man, was bad. What was he, in short, but a huge *sulky Dandy*; of giant dimensions, to be sure, yet still a Dandy; who sulked, as poor Mrs Hunt expressed it, "like a schoolboy that had got a plain bunn given him instead of a plum one." [Lord Byron] *CL 6.148* [To Macvey Napier]

Necessary Evil. [Carlyle's pet name for his wife] *JAF 3.345*

I see something of fashionable people here, and truly to my plebeian conception there is not a more futile class of persons on the face of the earth. *JAF 1.186*

Miss Martineau was here and is gone...broken into utter wearisomeness, a mind reduced to these three elements: Imbecility, Dogmatism, and Unlimited Hope. I never in my life was more heartily bored with any creature. [Harriet Martineau] *JAF 3.401*

That girl is an absolute fool — and it is a mercy for her that she is so ill-looking. [Geraldine Jewsbury] *S 190*

There was one of those public guardians there, whose throat I could have cut that night; his voice was loud, hideous, and ear and soul piercing, resembling the voices of ten thousand gib-cats all molten into one terrific peal. [On a public watchman] *JAF 1.202*

The Bullers are essentially a cold race of people. They live in the midst of fashion and external show. They love no living creature. *JAF 1.224*

Such is my conclusion with the Bullers. I feel glad that I have done with them; their family was ruining my mind and body. I was selling the very quintessence of my spirit for 200 pounds a year. Twelve months spent at Boulogne in the midst of drivelling and discomfort would have added little to my stock of cash, and fearfully diminished my remnant of spirits, health, and affection... Adieu, therefore, to ancient dames of quality, that flaunting, painting, patching, nervous, vapourish, jigging, skimming, scolding race of mortals. Their clothes are silk, their manners courtly, their hearts are *kipper*. *JAF 1.227-8*

When I think of General Dixon's brats, and how they used to vex me, I often wonder I had not broken their backs at once, and left them. *JAF 1.166*

I see what you are now — a damned impudent whelp of an Edinburgh advocate. [Mr Skirving.] *S 211*

My hearers were mixtiform dandiacal of both sexes, Drysadustical, ingenuous, ingenious, and grew, on the whole, more and more silent. [On the audience at one of his lectures] *JAF 3.108*

He is the nearest approach to an Incarnated Forty-seventh of Euclid that I ever saw walking. [John Stuart Mill] *CL 9.150* [To John A Carlyle]

A genuine man, which is much, but also essentially a small genuine man. [William Wordsworth] *JAF 3.31*

When I compare that man [Wordsworth] with a great man, alas! he is like dwindling into a contemptibility. Jean Paul [Richter], for example, could have worn him in a finger-ring. *JAF 3.31*

Bentham is a Denyer, he *denies* with a loud and universally convincing voice: his fault is that he can *affirm* nothing, except that money is pleasant in the purse, and food in the stomach, and that by this simplest of all Beliefs he can reorganise Society. [Jeremy Bentham] *CL 5.212* [To Macvey Napier]

The kind of man that Keats was gets ever more horrible to me. [John Keats] *JAF 3.450*

He sits in a cesspool and adds to it. [Algernon Swinburne] *W 6.138*

Hazlitt is writing his way thro' France and Italy: the ginshops and pawnbrokers bewail his absence. [William Hazlitt] *CL 3.234* [To Jane Baillie Welsh]

Poor fellow! he mistakes it for fame. He does not see that it is only an extended pillory that he is standing on. [Bishop Colenso] *JAF 4.263*

Mrs John Sterling is a heap of euphuistic affectations; very wearisome, with a shoal of loud children. *CL 10.17* [To John A Carlyle]

ON LITERATURE

How delicate, decent is English Biography, bless its mealy mouth. *Col 10.221* ['Sir Walter Scott']

I have felt in general as if I should like never to write any line more in the world. Literature! Oh Literature! Oh that Literature had never been devised! *JAF 3.120*

Printing, which comes necessarily out of writing, I say often, is equivalent to Democracy: invent Writing, Democracy is inevitable. *Col 12.194* [*On Heroes, Hero-Worship*]

Literature is but a branch of Religion, and always partakes in its character: however, in our time, it is the only branch that still shows any greenness; and, as some think, must one day become the main stem. *Col 8.353* ['Characteristics']

It is a damnable heresy in criticism to maintain either

expressly or implicitly that the ultimate object of poetry is sensation. That of cookery is such, but not that of poetry. *JAF 1.371*

Such is the literary world of London; indisputably the poorest part of its population at present. *JAF 1.264*

We are all poets when we read a poem well. *Col 12.97* [*On Heroes, Hero-Worship*]

Literature is the wine of life. It will not, cannot, be its food. What is it that makes blue-stockings of women, magazine hacks of men? They neglect household and social duties. They have no household and social enjoyments. Life is no longer with them a verdant field, but a *hortus siccus*. They exist pent up in noisome streets, amid feverish excitements. They despise or overlook the common blessedness which Providence has laid out for all his creatures, and try to substitute for it a distilled quintessence prepared in the alembic of painters and rhymers and sweet singers. What is the result? This ardent spirit parches up their nature. They become discontented and despicable, or wretched and dangerous. Byron and all strong souls go the latter

way. Campbell and all the weak souls the former...
Away! be men before attempting to be writers. *JAF
1.272*

The booksellers of the universe are bipeds of an erect
form and speak articulately; therefore they deserve the
name of men, and from me at least they shall always
get it. But for the rest, their thoughts are redolent of
"solid pudding." *JAF 1.295*

Milnes has written this year a book on Keats. This
remark to make on it; "An attempt to make us eat dead
dog by exquisite currying and cooking." Won't eat it.
A truly unwise little book. *JAF 3.450*

Empty as other folks' kettles are, artists' kettles are
emptier, and good for nothing but tying to the tails of
mad dogs. *S 241*

Literary men are....a perpetual priesthood. *Col 6.69*
['State of German Literature']

I struggled through the *Eikon Basiliske* yesterday; one of
the paltriest pieces of vapid, shovel-hatted, clear-

starched, immaculate falsity and cant I have ever read.
JAF 3.199

There is no heroic poem in the world but is at bottom a
biography, the life of a man: also, it may be said, there
is no life of a man, faithfully recorded, but is a heroic
poem of its sort, rhymed or unrhymed. *Col 10.218* ['Sir
Walter Scott']

You have lost nothing by missing the autobiography of
[John Stuart] Mill. I have never read a more
uninteresting book, nor I should say a sillier, by a man
of sense, integrity, and seriousness of mind... It is
wholly the life of a logic-chopping engine, little more
of human in it than if it had been done by a thing of
mechanized iron. Autobiography of a steam-engine,
perhaps, you may sometimes read it. *JAF 4.420*

Literature is the Thought of thinking Souls. *Col 10.281*
['Sir Walter Scott']

If any author can be reviewed to death, let it be, with
all possible despatch, *done*. *Col 9.85* ['Boswell's *Life of
Johnson*']

Look at the biography of authors! Except the Newgate Calendar, it is the most sickening chapter in the history of man. The calamities of these people are a fertile topic; and too often their faults and vices have kept pace with their calamities. *Col 5.52* [*The Life of Friedrich Schiller*]

What a sad want I am in of libraries, of books to gather facts from! Why is there not a Majesty's library in every county town? There is a Majesty's jail and gallows in every one. *JAF 2.281*

A well written Life in almost as rare as a well-spent one. *Col 6.3* ['Jean Paul Friedrich Richter']

One thing I imagine to be clear enough, that bookselling, slain by puffery, is dead, and will not come alive again, though worms may for some time live in the carcase. *JAF 2.278*

Literature, as a profession, is what I would counsel no faithful man to be concerned with, except when absolutely forced into it, under penalty, as it were, of death. *JAF 4.437*

There is a great discovery still to be made in Literature, that of paying literary men by the quantity they *do not* write. *Col 10.218* ['Sir Walter Scott']

The true University of these days is a Collection of Books. *Col 12.192* [*On Heroes, Hero-Worship*]

Close thy *Byron*; open thy *Goethe*. *Col 1.184* [*Sartor Resartus*]

I find on a general view that the book is one of the savagest written for several centuries. It is a book written by a wild man, a man disunited from the fellowship of the world he lives in. [On his *History of the French Revolution*.] *JAF 3.96*

A poet without love were a physical and metaphysical impossibility. *Col 7.29* ['Burns']

There is something in reading a dull book very nauseous to me. *JAF 1.198*

On all sides, are we not driven to the conclusion that, of all the things which man can do or make here below, by far the most momentous, wonderful and worthy are the things we call Books! *Col 12.195* [*On Heroes, Hero-Worship*]

Books are like men's souls; divided into sheep and goats. *Col 11.315* ['Inaugural Address']

Books born mostly of Chaos — which want all things, even an *Index* — are a painful object. *Col 21.14* [*Frederick the Great*]

Lord Bacon could have easily have created the planets as he could have written *Hamlet*. [*Attr.*]

Four books Mr C[roker] had by him, wherefrom to gather light for the fifth, which was Boswell's. What does he do but now, in the placidest manner, — slit the whole five into slips, and sew these together into a sextum quid, exactly at his own convenience: giving Boswell the credit of the whole! By what art-magic, our readers ask, has he united them? By the simplest of all: by Brackets. Never before was the full virtue of the Bracket made manifest. You begin a sentence under Boswell's guidance, thinking to be carried happily through it by the same: but no, in the middle, perhaps after a semi-colon, and some consequent 'for', — starts up one of those Bracket-ligatures, and stitches you in from half a page to twenty or thirty pages of a Hawkins, Tyers, Murphy, Piozzi; so that one must make the old sad reflection, where we are, we know, whither we are going, no man knoweth! *Col 9.31* ['Boswell's *Life of Johnson*']

The Printing Press is the only, or by far the chief, Pulpit in these days. *CL 15.160* [To John Sterling]

Few Englishmen can make the smallest attempt at writing Biography: they are a poor mode-ridden and otherwise hag-ridden people; hunting after Respectability, in perpetual terror of missing it; and so write, as they do all other things, in a state of partial paralysis. *CL 6.263* [To John Stuart Mill]

Money cannot hire the writing of a book, but it can the printing of it. *JAF 2.285*

His silence is more eloquent than words. [Dante] *Col 12.109* [*On Heroes, Hero-Worship*]

ON POLITICS

There shall be Free Trade, in all senses, and to all lengths: unlimited Free Trade — which some take to mean "Free racing, ere long with unlimited speed, in the career of *Cheap and Nasty.*" *Col 11.340* ['Shooting Niagara: and After']

All political follies issue at last in a broken head to somebody. *JAF 4.448*

Find in any country the Ablest Man that exists there; raise *him* to the supreme place, and loyally reverence him; you have a perfect government for that country; no ballot-box, parliamentary eloquence, voting, constitution-building, or other machinery whatsoever can improve it a whit. *Col 12.234* [*On Heroes, Hero-Worship*]

It is the everlasting privilege of the foolish to be governed by the wise. *Col 19.28* [*Latter-Day Pamphlets*]

I say, Find me the true *Könning*, King, or able-man, and he has a divine right over me. *Col 12.237* [*On Heroes, Hero-Worship*]

And in saying that, I am but saying in other words that we are in an epoch of anarchy. Anarchy *plus* a constable! *Col 11.329* ['Inaugural Address']

Burke said that there were Three Estates in Parliament; but, in the Reporters' Gallery yonder, there sat a *Fourth Estate*, more important far than they all. *Col 12.194* [*On Heroes, Hero-Worship*]

Vain hope, to make people happy by politics! *JAF 2.206*

If, at any time, a philosophy of Laissez-faire, Competition and Supply-and-Demand, start up as the exponent of human relations, expect that it will soon end. *Col 13.235* [*Past and Present*]

Is it true that of all quacks that ever quacked in any age of the world the political economists of this age are, for their intrinsic size, the loudest? Mercy on us, what a quack-quacking; and their egg, even if not a wind one, is of value simply one half-penny. *JAF 2.73*

When we can drink the Ocean into mill-ponds, and bottle up the force of Gravity, to be sold retail, in gas-jars; then may we hope to comprehend the infinitudes of man's soul under formulas of Profit and Loss. *Col 7.330* ['Signs of the Times']

Supply-and-demand is not the one Law of Nature; Cash-payment is not the sole nexus of man with man. *Col 13.232* [*Past and Present*]

A good structure of legislation, a proper check upon the executive, a wise arrangement of the judiciary is all that is wanting for human happiness. *Col 7.325* ['Signs of the Times']

If there can be no reform of Downing Street, I care not much for the reform of Parliament. *Col 19.298* [*Latter-Day Pamphlets*]

All reform except a moral one will prove unavailing. *Col 19.204* [*Latter-Day Pamphlets*]

The mass of men consulted at hustings, upon any high matter whatsoever, is as ugly an exhibition of human stupidity as this world sees. *Col 19.291* [*Latter-Day Pamphlets*]

With what serene conclusiveness a member of some Useful Knowledge Society stops your mouth with a figure of arithmetic. *Col 10.333* [*Chartism*]

A man with £200,000 a year eats the whole fruit of 6666 men's labour through a year; for you can get a stout spadesman to work and maintain himself for the sum of £30. Thus we have private individuals whose wages are equal to the wages of seven or eight thousand other individuals. What do those highly beneficed individuals do to society for their wages? — Kill partridges. CAN this last? No, by the soul that is in man it cannot, and will not, and shall not! *JAF 2.83*

The Working Aristocracy — Yes, but on the threshold of all this, it is again and again to be asked, What of the Idle Aristocracy? Again and again, What shall we say of the Idle Aristocracy, the owners of the soil of England; whose recognised function is that of handsomely consuming the rents of England, shooting the partridges of England, and as an agreeable amusement (if the purchase-money and other conveniences serve), dilettante-ing in Parliament and Quarter-Sessions for England? We will say mournfully, in the presence of Heaven and Earth,— that we stand speechless, stupent, and know not what to say! *Col 13.222* [*Past and Present*]

Surely Honourable Members ought to speak of the Condition-of-England question too. *Col 10.328* [*Chartism*]

But how different when it is with arguments you fight! Here no victory yet definable can be considered as final. Beat him down with Parliamentary invective, till sense be fled; cut him in two, hanging one half on this dilemma-horn, the other on that; blow the brains or thinking-faculty quite out of him for the time: it skills not; he rallies and revives on the morrow; tomorrow he repairs his golden fires! The thing that *will* logically extinguish him is perhaps still a desideratum in Constitutional civilisation. For how, till a man know, in some measure, at what point he becomes logically defunct, can Parliamentary Business be carried on, and Talk cease or slake? *Col 3.20-1* [*The French Revolution*]

How my Prime Minister was appointed is of less moment to me than How my House Servant was hired. *Col 9.47* ['Boswell's *Life of Johnson*']

I do not take the smallest interest in what is called "Public Business," Politics, &c &c — which in fact is rather "Public Idleness with Noise." Let them jar away there; they *"can di' tha naither ill na' guid."* *CL 8.296* [To Jean Carlyle Aitken]

Social science... what we might call, by way of eminence, the *dismal science*. *Col 11.177* ['The Nigger Question']

ON HISTORY AND SCIENCE

I thought that it was the abolition of rubbish. I find it has been only the kindling of a dunghill. The dry straw on the outside burns off; but the huge damp rotting mass remains where it was. [On the French Revolution.] *JAF 2.54*

Always an unruly fellow, and dangerous to trust among crockery. [Friedrich Wilhelm.] *Col 21.38* [*Frederick the Great*]

No great man lives in vain. The History of the world is but the Biography of great men. *Col 12.34* [*On Heroes, Hero-Worship*]

History, a distillation of rumour. *Col 2.319* [*The French Revolution*]

History is the essence of innumerable Biographies. *Col 7.348* ['On History']

It is not speaking with exaggeration, but with strict measured sobriety, to say that this Book of Boswell's will give more real insight into the History of England during those days than twenty other Books, falsely entitled 'Histories'. *Col 9.45* ['Boswell's *Life of Johnson*']

Alas, what mountains of dead ashes, wreck and burnt bones, does assiduous Pedantry dig up from the Past Time, and name it History; till, as we say, the human soul sinks wearied and bewildered; till the Past Time seems all one infinite incredible gray void, without sun, stars, hearth-fires, or candle-light; dim offensive dust-whirlwinds filling universal Nature; and over your Historical Library, it is as if all the Titans had written for themselves: DRY RUBBISH SHOT HERE! *Col 13.61* [*Past and Present*]

It shall be such a book: quite an epic poem of the Revolution: an apotheosis of Sanscullotism! [On his *History of the French Revolution*.] *JAF 2.456*

To me, it often seems, as if the right *History* (that impossible thing I mean by History) of the French Revolution were the grand Poem of our Time; as if the man who *could* write the *truth* of that, were worth all other writers and singers. *CL 6.446* [To John Stuart Mill]

Never read a Book of History *without a map*. Follow out the details of the localities (chronologies &c &c): it *forces* you to pay a livelier attention;—till you have put the event into its *place* and into its *time*, in every detail, you cannot be said to have read it at all. *CL 25.194* [To William Allingham]

I finished last night the dullest thick book, long-winded, though intelligent, of Lyell; and the tendency of it, very impotent, was, upon the whole, to prove that we are much the same as the apes; that Adam was probably no other than a fortunate ourang-outang who succeeded in rising in the world. May the Lord confound all such dreary insolences of loquacious blockheadism, entitling itself Science. *JAF 4.288*

Nature abhors a vacuum — worthy old girl! *JAF 3.172*

I will add only one other word; about Physiology: do not study that for such a purpose; it has no light for you, but darkness visible, the thing they call Physiology at present. "Science falsely so called!" Man's Body too, is it not "a *garment* woven in the loom of Heaven?" I mean that scientifically; in spite of all royal societies, that is the very truth of it. My right hand is miraculous to me (were I not stupid of heart), as miraculous as a soul made visible — *is*; as a ghost rising from the dead would be. Consider what is your right hand. Were there only *one* right hand in the world! On the whole, you will see by and by that "Materialism" is but a black spectral Illusion, — to be looked at, with brave eyes, and then it vanishes, owns itself to be Nothing. *CL 12.165* [To Geraldine Jewsbury]

It is a mathematical fact that the casting of this pebble from my hand alters the centre of gravity of the Universe. *Col 1.238* [*Sartor Resartus*]

MAXIMS
AND
OBSERVATIONS ON LIFE

No man who has once heartily and wholly laughed can be altogether irreclaimably bad. *Col 1.32* [*Sartor Resartus*]

I never heard tell of any clever man that came of entirely stupid people. *Col 11.313* ['Inaugural Address']

No man, it has been said, is a hero to his valet; and this is probably true; but the fault is at least as likely to be the valet's as the hero's. *Col 7.4* ['Burns']

The first duty for a man is still that of subduing *Fear*. *Col 12.37* [*On Heroes, Hero-Worship*]

The greatest of faults, I should say, is to be conscious of none. *Col 12.56* [*On Heroes, Hero-Worship*]

Strength, well understood, is the measure of all worth.

give a thing time; if it can succeed, it is a right thing. *Y 174*

For true Strength is one and the same with Beauty, and its worship is also a hymn. *Col 7.337* ['Signs of the Times']

Deeds are greater than words. *Col 13.201* [*Past and Present*]

It is shrewdly guessed that where there is great preaching there will be little almsgiving. *Col 8.337* ['Characteristics']

The fever-fire of Ambition is too painfully extinguished in the frost-bath of Poverty. *Col 9.62* ['Boswell's *Life of Johnson*']

Were a pair of breeches ever known to beget a son? *JAF 3.193*

Great is self denial! *JAF 2.307*

Man is a Tool-using Animal. *Col 1.39* [*Sartor Resartus*]

Attempt not the impossibility to 'know thyself', but solely 'to know that thou canst work at.' *JAF 2.270*

Silence is deep as Eternity, speech is shallow as Time. *Col 10.218* ['Sir Walter Scott']

Let us have the crisis: we shall either have death or the cure. *Col 12.204* [*On Heroes, Hero-Worship*]

Great men are too often unknown, or, what is worse, misknown. *Col 1.16* [*Sartor Resartus*]

The barrenest of all mortals is the sentimentalist. *Col 8.338* ['Characteristics']

Of all outward evils Obscurity is perhaps in itself the least. *Col 9.84* ['Boswell's *Life of Johnson*']

How much has been concealed, how much has been defended in Aprons! *Col 1.41* [*Sartor Resartus*]

Fancy that thou deservest to be hanged (as is most likely), thou wilt feel it happiness to be only shot. *Col 1.184* [*Sartor Resartus*]

Loud clamour is always more or less insane. *Col 9.87* ['Boswell's *Life of Johnson*']

The tolerance of others is but doubt and indifference. *JAF 3.127*

Your rusty kettle will continue to boil your water for you if you don't try to mend it. Begin tinkering, and there is an end of your kettle. *JAF 4.450*

Is not Sentimentalism the twin sister to Cant, if not one and the same with it. *Col 2.67* [*The French Revolution*]

Clever men are good, but they are not the best. *Col 6.292* ['Goethe']

He that has done nothing can know nothing. Vain is it to sit scheming and plausibly discoursing: up and be doing! *Col 9.185* ['Corn-Law Rhymes']

To a shower of gold most things are penetrable. *Col 2.123* [*The French Revolution*]

Rest is for the dead. *Journal Jun 22 1830*

Whoso belongs only to his own age, and reverences only its gilt Popinjays or soot-smeared Mumbojumbos, must needs die with it. *Col 9.55* ['Boswell's *Life of Johnson*']

What is man? An omnivorous Biped that wears Breeches. *Col 1.64* [*Sartor Resartus*]

With Stupidity and sound Digestion man may front much. *Col 1.157* [*Sartor Resartus*]

They that will crowd about bonfires may, sometimes very fairly, get their beards singed; it is the price they pay for such illumination. *Col 10.223* ['Sir Walter Scott']

You cannot fight the battle in dressing-gown and slippers. *CL 6.258* [To John Stuart Mill]

A man cannot make a pair of shoes rightly unless he do it in a devout manner. *JAF 3.277*

But the world is an old woman, and mistakes any gilt farthing for a gold coin; whereby being often cheated, she will thenceforth trust nothing but the common copper. *Col 1.122* [*Sartor Resartus*]

No man lives without jostling and being jostled; in all ways he has to *elbow* himself through the world, giving and receiving offence. *Col 10.222* ['Sir Walter Scott']

No man sees far; the most see no farther than their noses. *Col 9.342* ['Count Cagliostro']

Fancy that thou deservest to be hanged (as is most likely), thou wilt feel it happiness to be only shot: fancy that thou deservest to be hanged in a hair-halter, it will be a luxury to die in hemp. *Col 1.184* [*Sartor Resartus*]

Thus do Men and Sheep play their parts on this Nether Earth; wandering restlessly in large masses, they know not whither; for most part, each following his neighbour, and his own nose. *Col 9.53* ['Boswell's *Life of Johnson*']

Of Geology and Geognesy we know enough; what with the labours of our Werners and Huttons, what with the ardent genius of their disciples, it has come about that now, to many a Royal Society, the Creation of a World is little more mysterious than the cooking of a Dumpling; concerning which last, indeed, there have been minds to whom the question, *How the Apples were got in*, presented difficulties. *Col 1.3-4* [*Sartor Resartus*]

The fraction of life can be increased in value not so much by increasing your Numerator as by lessening your Denominator. *Col 1.184* [*Sartor Resartus*]

Human creatures will not *go* quite accurately together, any more than clocks will. *Col 21.58* [*Frederick the Great*]

What a noisy inanity is this world. *JAF 2.469*

The works of a man, bury them under what guano-mountains and obscene owl-droppings you will, do not perish, cannot perish. *Col 18.171* [*Oliver Cromwell's Letters and Speeches*]

I wish she could once get it fairly into her head that neither woman nor man, nor any kind of creature in this universe, was born for the exclusive, or even for the chief, purpose of falling in love, or being fallen in love with. *JAF 3.216*

I am for permanence in all things, at the earliest possible moment, and to the latest possible. *Col 13.345* [*Past and Present*]

On the whole, too, it is worth considering what element your Quack specially works in: the element of wonder! The Genuine, be he artist or artisan, works in the finitude of the Known; the Quack in the infinitude of the Unknown. *Col 9.364-5* ['Count Cagliostro']

Depend upon it, for one thing, good Reader, no age ever seemed the Age of Romance to *itself*. *Col 10.6* ['The Diamond Necklace']

God keep us all, I pray again, from the madness of popularity. I never knew one whom it did not injure. I have known strong men whom it killed. *JAF 3.100*

What is a man if you look at him with the mere logical sense, with the understanding? A pitiful hungry biped that wears breeches. Often when I read of pompous ceremonials, drawing room levées, and coronations, on a sudden the clothes fly off the whole party in my fancy, and they stand there straddling in a half ludicrous half horrid condition! *JAF 2.85*

Might and Right do differ frightfully from hour to hour; but give them centuries to try it in, they are found to be identical. *Col 10.389* [*Chartism*]

The scoundrel needs no protection. The scoundrel that *will* hasten to the gallows, why not rather clear the way for him! *Col 19.80* [*Latter-Day Pamphlets*]

All the Dukes in creation melted into one Duke were not worth sixpence to me. *JAF 3.251*

If the Devil some good night should take his hammer and smite in shivers all and every piano of our European world, so that in broad Europe there were not one piano left soundable, would the harm be great? Would not, on the contrary, the relief be considerable? *JAF 3.266*

Alas, all the world is a "republic of mediocrities," and

always was. *CL 28.135* [To Ralph Waldo Emerson]

Heroes have gone-out; Quacks have come-in. *Col 12.206* [*On Heroes, Hero-Worship*]

A big bag of wind and nothingness. [Wellington's funeral] *JAF 4.125*

The car or hearse, a monstrous bronze mass, which broke through the pavement in various places, its weight being seven or ten tons, was of all the objects I ever saw the abominably ugliest, or nearly so. An incoherent huddle of expensive palls, flags, sheets, and gilt emblems and cross poles, more like one of the street carts that hawk door-mats than a bier for a hero. Disgust was general at this vile *ne plus ultra* of Cockneyism. [Wellington's funeral] *JAF 4.126*

German, to this day, is a frightful dialect for the stupid, the pedant and dullard sort! *Col 21.398* [*Frederick the Great*]

Several months ago, some friends took me with them to see one of the London Prisons; a Prison of the exemplary or model kind... in my life I never saw so clean a building; probably no Duke in England lives in a mansion of such perfect and thorough cleanness. *Col 19.63-4* [*Latter-Day Pamphlets*]

Irving and she are sometimes ridiculous enough at present in the matter of their son, a quiet wersh gorb of a thing, as all children of six weeks are, but looked upon by them as if it were a cherub from on high. The concerns of 'him' (as they emphatically call it) occupy a large share of public attention. Kitty Kirkpatrick smiles covertly, and I laugh aloud at the earnest devotedness of the good Orator to this weighty affair. 'Isabella', said he the other night, 'I would wash him, I think with warm water tonight,' a counsel received with approving assent by the mother, but somewhat objected to by others. I declared the washing and dressing of him to be the wife's concern alone; and that, were I in her place, I would wash him with oil of vitriol if I pleased, and take no one's counsel in it. *JAF 1.242*

Alas, go where you will, especially in these irreverent ages, the noteworthy Dead is sure to be found lying under infinite dung, no end of calumnies and stupidities accumulated upon him. *Col 21.18* [*Frederick the Great*]

So I say of dinner popularity, lords and lionism — Keep it; give it to those that like it. *JAF 3.187*

Revenge, my friends! revenge, and the natural hatred of scoundrels, and the ineradical tendency to *revancher* oneself upon them, and pay them what they have merited; this is forevermore intrinsically a correct, and even a divine feeling in the mind of every man. *Col 19.94* [*Latter-Day Pamphlets*]

That is the way of female intellects when they are good; nothing equals their acuteness, and their rapidity is almost excessive. *Col 21.53-4* [*Frederick the Great*]

Law, I fear, must be renounced; it is a shapeless mass of absurdity and chicane. *S 51*

The Public is an old woman: let her maunder and mumble. *CL 9.228* [To John Sterling]

A day of justice, when the worth of Breeches would be revealed to man, and the scissors become forever venerable. *Col 1.281* [*Sartor Resartus*]

Lives the man that can figure a naked Duke of Windlestraw addressing a naked House of Lords? *Col 1.60* [*Sartor Resartus*]

Decidedly the most insufferable picture that has yet been made of me, a delerious-looking mountebank full of violence, awkwardness, atrocity, and stupidity, without recognisable likeness to anything I have ever known in any feature of me. [On a portrait by John Everett Millais.] *JAF 4.380*

All that's very interesting, Darwin, no doubt; how we men were evolved from apes and all that, and perhaps true....but what I want to know is how we're to prevent this present generation from devolving into apes? [*Attr.* Frank Harris]

How has our head on the outside a polished Hat... and in the inside Vacancy, or a froth of Vocables and Attorney-Logic! *Col 1.115* [*Sartor Resartus*]

We seem to me a People so enthralled and buried under bondage to the Hearsays and the Cants and the Grimaces, as no People ever were before. Literally so. From the top of our Metropolitan Cathedral to the sill of our lowest Cobbler's shop, it is to me, too often, like one general *somnabulism*, most strange, most miserable,— most damnable! *CL 21.240* [To Robert Browning]

Maid-servants, I hear people complaining, are getting instructed in the "ologies," and are apparently becoming more and more ignorant of brewing, hailing, and baking. *Col 11.320* ['Inaugural Address']

Which of your Philosophical Systems is other than a dream-theorem; a net quotient, confidently given out, where divisor and dividend are both unknown? *Col 1.51* [*Sartor Resartus*]

We have quietly closed our eyes to the eternal Substance of things, and opened them only to the Shows and Shams of things. We quietly believe this Universe to be intrinsically a great unintelligible PERHAPS. *Col 13.171* [*Past and Present*]

The crash of the whole Solar and Stellar System could only kill you *once*. *CL 6.53* [To John A Carlyle]

Life everywhere is the most manageable matter, simple as a question in the Rule-of-Three: multiply your second and third term together, divide the product by the first, and your quotient will be the answer, — which you are but an ass if you cannot come at. The booby has not yet found-out, by any trial, that, do what one will, there is ever a cursed fraction, oftenest a decimal repeater, and no net integer quotient so much as to be thought of. *Col 1.125-6* [*Sartor Resartus*]

For is not every meanest day, the confluence of two Eternities? *Col 2.168* [*The French Revolution*]

See deep enough, and you see musically; the heart of Nature *being* everywhere music, if you can only reach it. *Col 12.99* [*On Hero, Hero-Worship*]

There is no kind of achievement you could make in the world that is equal to perfect health. *Col 11.330* ['Inaugural Address']

If man's Soul is indeed, as in the Finnish Language, and Utilitarian Philosophy, a kind of *Stomach*, what else is the true meaning of Spiritual Union but an Eating together? Thus we, instead of Friends, are Dinner-guests. *Col 1.116* [*Sartor Resartus*]

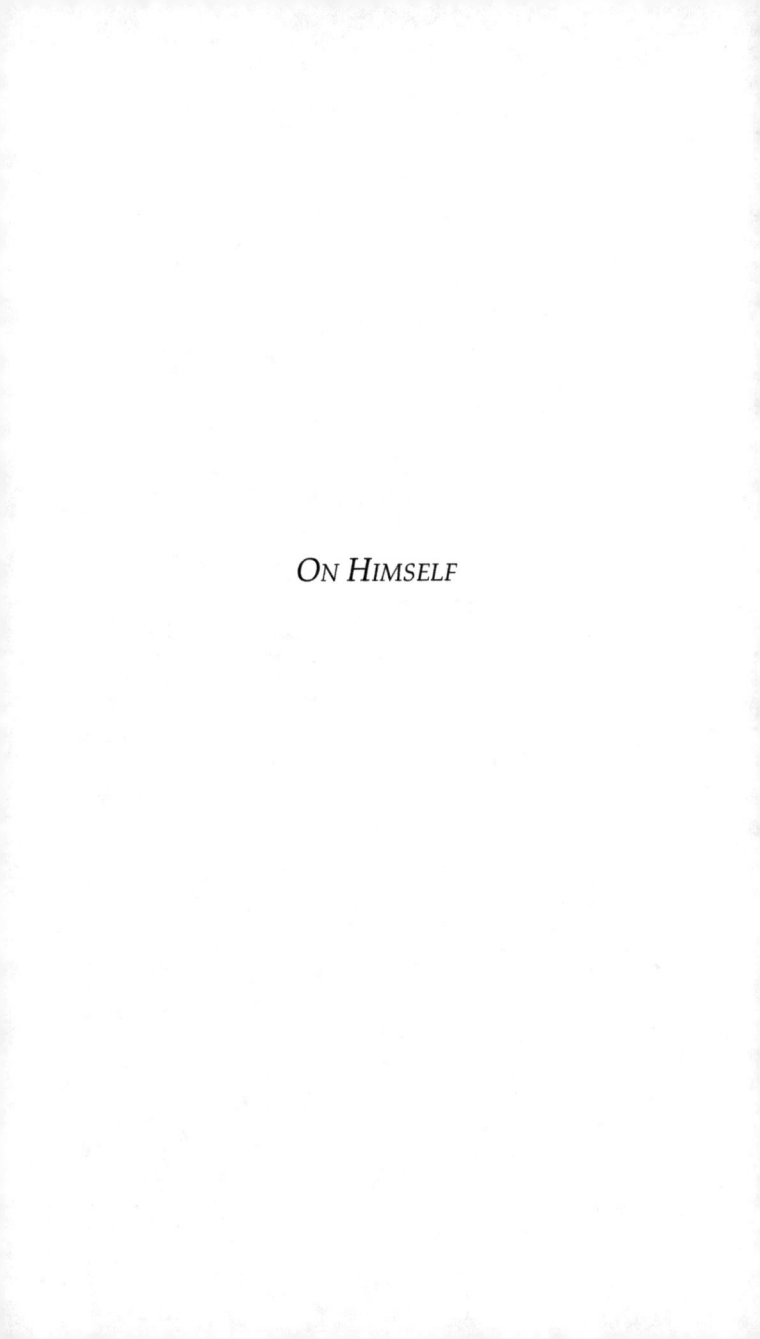

ON HIMSELF

Often, very often, I think, "Would the human species universally be but so kind as to leave me altogether alone!" *JAF 3.450*

To me the universe was all void of life, of purpose, of volition, even of hostility; it was one huge, dead, immeasurable steam-engine, rolling on in its dead indifference, to grind me limb from limb. Oh, the vast, gloomy, solitary Golgotha and mill of death! *JAF 1.105*

Thus had the Everlasting No pealed authoritatively through all the recesses of my Being, of my ME; and then was it that my whole ME stood up, in native God-created majesty, and with emphasis recorded its Protest. Such a Protest, the most important transaction in my Life, may that same Indignation and Defiance, in a psychological point of view, be fitly called. The Everlasting No had said: "Behold, thou art fatherless, outcast, and the Universe is mine (the Devil's);" to which my whole ME now made answer; "I am not thine but Free, and forever hate thee!"

It is from this hour that I incline to date my Spiritual New-birth, or Baphometic Fire-baptism; perhaps I directly thereupon began to be a Man. *Col 1.163* [*Sartor Resartus*]

The day before yesterday his Prussian Excellency forwarded to me by registered parcel all the documents and insignia connected with our sublime elevation to the Prussian Order of Merit. Due reply sent; and so we have done, thank heaven, with this sublime nonentity. I feel about it, after the fact is over, quite as emphatically as I did at first — that had they sent me a quarter of a pound of good tobacco, the addition to my happiness would probably have been suitabler and greater. *JAF 4.425*

I do hold it, in my own case, a kind of disgrace and crime to be sick. *CL 9.68* [To John Sterling]

In fact as I grow older I grow more careless about appointments: Keep them, Gentlemen; I will do without them. *CL 8.310* [To John A Carlyle]

I declare solemnly, without exaggeration, that I impute nine-tenths of present wretchedness, and rather more than nine-tenths of all my faults, to this infernal disorder on the stomach. [On his indigestion] *JAF 1.200*

Nay on certain points I even ask my horse's opinion. *Col 19.293* [*Latter-Day Pamphlets*]

I do not believe in 'Art' — nay, I do believe it to be one of the deadliest cants. *JAF 3.421*

I feel I am not master of the *haut ton* of intercourse. *S 54*

Nothing spurs me but an evil conscience. *JAF 2.280*

To reform a world, to reform a nation, no wise man will undertake; and all but foolish men know, that the only solid, though a far slower reformation, is what each begins and perfects on *himself*. *Col 7.342* ['Signs of the Times']

I have wandered thro' long dreary years in endless

mazes of Speculation till my whole heart was sick; and hung sorites on sorites; and ended ever in Inanity: till at length the whole business was happily swept to the right and the left, and I found with amazement that the thing I wanted was not Telescopes and Optical Diagrams but *Eyes* and things to see with them. *CL 6.403* [To John Stuart Mill]

What you ask about my likeness in the Exhibition is unanswerable: the thing belongs to one Lawrence, a young artist of great promise as yet all unripe... I likened it, four months ago when I struck work in sitting, to a compound of the head of a Demon and of a Flayed Horse; *infandum, infandum. CL 13.208* [To John Sterling]

No more abominable blotch, without one feature of mine, was ever called by the name of a rational man. It is the portrait of an idiot that has taken Glauber salts and lost his eyesight. [On another portrait] *JAF 4.76*

ON RELIGION

He who would understand to what a pass Catholicism, and much else, had now got; and how the symbols of the Holiest have become gambling-dice of the basest — must read the narrative of those things by Besenval, and Soulavie, and the other Court Newsmen of the time. He will see the Versailles Galaxy all scattered asunder, grouped into new ever-shifting Constellations. There are nods and sagacious glances; go-betweens, silk dowagers mysteriously gliding, with smiles for this constellation, sighs for that; there is tremor, of hope or desperation, in several hearts. There is the pale grinning Shadow of Death, ceremoniously ushered along by another grinning Shadow, of Etiquette: at intervals the growl of Chapel Organs, like prayer by machinery; proclaiming, as in a kind of horrid diabolic horse-laughter, *Vanity of vanities, all is Vanity! Col 2.21* [*The French Revolution*]

I am neither Pagan nor Turk, not circumcised Jew, but

an unfortunate Christian individual resident at Chelsea in *this* year of Grace; neither Pantheist or Pot-theist, nor any Theist or *ist* whatsoever; having the most decided contempt for all manner of System-builders and Sect-founders.   *CL 8.137* [To John Sterling]

I dare say you have not seen in the newspapers, but will soon see something extraordinary about poor Edward Irving. His friends here are all much grieved about him, For many months he has been puddling and muddling in the midst of certain insane jargonings of hysterical women, and crack-brained enthusiasts, who start up from time to time in public companies, and utter confused stuff, mostly "Ohs" and "Ahs", and absurd interjections about "the body of Jesus"; they also pretend to "work miracles", and have raised more than one weak bed-rid woman, and cured people of "nerves", or as they themselves say, "cast devils out of them". All which poor Irving is pleased to consider as the "work of the Spirit", and to janner about at great length, as making his church the peculiarly blessed of Heaven, and equal to or greater than the primitive one at Corinth. This, greatly to my sorrow and that of many, has gone on privately a good while, with increasing vigour; but, last Sabbath it burst out publicly in the open church; for one of the "Prophetesses", a woman on the verge of derangement, started up in the time of worship, and began to speak with tongues, and, as the thing was encouraged by Irving, there were some three or four fresh hands who started up in the evening sermon and began their ragings; whereupon the whole congregation got into foul uproar, some groaning, some laughing, some shrieking, not a few falling into swoons: more like a Bedlam than a Christian church. *JAF 2.213*

I had a letter from Edward Irving the other day about the Aesthetical Professorship in the London University... "The Lord," he says, blesses him: his Church rejoices in "the Lord"; in fact, the Lord and he seem to be quite hand and glove. *CL 4.253* [To John A Carlyle]

We also can read the Koran; our Translation of it, by Sale, is known to be a very fair one. I must say, it is as toilsome reading as I ever undertook. A wearisome confused jumble, crude, incondite, endless iterations, long-windedness, entanglement; most crude, incondite;— insupportable stupidity, in short! *Col 12.76* [*On Heroes, Hero-Worship*]

The three great elements of modern civilisation, Gunpowder, Printing, and the Protestant Religion. *Col 6.36* ['State of German Literature']

The poor old Church of England believes in no damnation except ruin at the bankers. [*Attr.*]

Scepticism writing about Belief may have great gifts; but it is really *ultra vires* there. It is Blindness laying-down the Laws of Optics. *Col 12.277* [*On Heroes, Hero-Worship*]

Scottish Puritanism, well considered, seems to me distinctly the noblest and completest form that the grand Sixteenth Century Reformation anywhere assumed. *K 145*

This country has been tolerably cleared of Jesuits proper; nor is there danger of their ever coming to a head here again. But, alas, the expulsion of the Jesuit Body avails us little, when the Jesuit *Soul* has so nestled itself in the life of mankind everywhere. *Col 19.263* [*Latter-Day Pamphlets*]

When I was reading Balmer's sermon on the Resurrection, it brought into my mind a sermon preached by Mr William Glen nearly on the same subject. He said many things about eternity of the body that would rise at the day of judgement, and the subject was disputed about by Robert Scott and George MacIvin. Robert Scott was for the same body rising again. The arguments were talked over one morning at the meeting house door. I was present, and was rather involved in the dispute. I observed that I thought a stinking clogg of a body like Robert Scott the weaver's would be very unfit to inhabit those places. *JAF 1.177*

I tried various chapels; I found in each some vulgar illiterate man declaiming about matters of which he knew nothing. I tried the Church of England. I found there a decent educated gentleman reading out of a book words very beautiful which had expressed once the sincere thoughts of pious admirable souls. I decidedly preferred the Church of England man, but I had to say to him: "I perceive, sir, that at the bottom you know as little about the matter as the other fellow." *JAF 3.44*

No man becomes a Saint in his sleep. *Col 13.67* [*Past and Present*]

Then, we have Religious machines, of all imaginable varieties; the Bible-Society, professing a far higher and heavenly structure, is found, on inquiry, to be altogether an earthly contrivance: supported by collection of moneys, by fomenting of vanities, by puffing, intrigue and chicane; a machine for converting the Heathen. *Col 7.318* ['Signs of the Times']

Has any man, or any society of men, a truth to speak, a piece of spiritual work to do; they can nowise proceed at once and with the mere natural organs, but must first call a public meeting, appoint committees, issue prospectuses, eat a public dinner. *Col 7.319* ['Signs of the Times']

Sect founders are a class I do not like. No truly great

man, from Jesus Christ downwards, ever founded a sect. *CL 15.193* [To Ralph Waldo Emerson]

If Jesus Christ were to come today, people wouldn't even crucify him. They would ask him to dinner, and hear what he had to say, and make fun of it. [*Attr.*]

It is a very fine pagoda if ye could get any sort of a God to put in it! [Cologne cathedral] *JAF 4.13*

On the whole, I often meditate on Christian things; but find as good as no profit in talking of them here. Most so-called Christians treat me instead with jargon of metaphysic formulas, or perhaps shovelhatted Coleridgian moonshine. *CL 8.306* [To John A Carlyle]

Of all *Antigigmen* too, in any time in any place, the greatest is that divine Hero of St Matthew. *CL 7.23* [To John Stuart Mill]

But surely in all Religions hitherto recognized, one indispensable element, and the essence of the whole, was this: *Some SYMBOL or Symbolic Representation, whereby the Divinity was sensibly manifested*. The Symbol may be the rudest, as in a Scandinavian Idol, an African Mumbo-jumbo; or it may be the highest, and of infinite significance, as Jesus of Nazareth, and his *Life*, and his *Biography*, and what followed therefrom: In all cases, there must *some* Symbol offer itself to the worshipper; for hereby alone is Imagination, the true organ of the Infinite in man, brought to harmonize with Understanding the organ of the Finite. *CL 5.278* [To Gustave D'Eichthal]

How different, above all, is that honey-mouthed, tear-stained, soup-kitchen Jesus Christ of our poor shovel-hatted modern Christians from that stern-visaged Christ of the Gospels, proclaiming aloud in the marketplace (with such a total contempt of the social respectabilities): "*Woe* unto you, Scribes and Pharisees, *hypocrites*"! Descend from your Gigs, ye wretched scoundrels, for the hour is come! *CL 6.443* [To John Stuart Mill]

ON PEOPLE AND PLACE

Edinburgh continues one of the dullest and poorest, and, on the whole, paltriest of places for me. I cannot remember that I have heard one sentence with true meaning in it uttered since I came hither. The very power of thought seems to have forsaken this Athenian city; at least, a more entirely shallow, barren, unfruitful, and trivial set of persons than those I meet with, never, that I remember, came across my bodily vision. *JAF 2.336*

This accursed, stinking, reeky mass of stones and lime and dung. [Edinburgh] *CL 1.324* [To John A Carlyle]

I have no interest to inform myself about the births in Annan, and care not if the process of birth and generation there should cease and determine altogether. *S 38*

It is noteworthy that the nobles of the country

[Scotland] have maintained a quite despicable behaviour from the times of Wallace downwards. A selfish, ferocious, famishing, unprincipled set of hyenas; from whom at no time and in no way has the country derived any benefit. *JAF 2.88*

Kildare, as I entered it, looked worse and worse — one of the wretchedest wild villages I ever saw, and full of ragged beggars: exotic, altogether like a village in Dahomey, man and church both. Knots of worshipping people hung about the streets, and everywhere round them hovered a harpy swarm of clamorous mendicants — men, women, children; a village winged, as if a flight of harpies had alighted on it. Here for the first time was Irish beggary itself. *JAF 4.3*

The whole country [Ireland] figures in my mind like a ragged coat; one huge beggar's gaberdine, not patched or patchable any longer. *JAF 4.21*

France was long a 'Despotism tempered by Epigrams,' and now, it would seem, the Epigrams have got the upper hand. *Col 2.50* [*The French Revolution*]

Remedy for Ireland? To cease generally from following the Devil! *JAF 4.7*

Of all the Nations in the world at present the English are the stupidest in speech, the wisest in action. *Col 13.200* [*Past and Present*]

Torpid, gluttonous, sooty, swollen, and squalid England is grown a phenomenon which fills me with disgust and apprehension, almost desperate, so far as it is concerned. What a base, pot-bellied blockhead this our heroic nation has become; sunk in its own dirty fat and offal, and of a stupidity defying the very gods. *JAF 4.399*

Alas, poor England! stupid, purblind, pudding-eating England! *JAF 2.90*

Twenty-seven millions mostly fools. [On the population of England] *Col 19.272* [*Latter-Day Pamphlets*]

Woe for us if we had nothing but what we can *show*, or speak. Silence, the great Empire of Silence; higher than the Stars; deeper than the Kingdoms of Death! It alone is great; all else is small. I hope we English will long maintain our *grand talent pour le silence*. *Col 12.265* [*On Heroes, Hero-Worship*]

All London-born men, without exception, seem to be narrow built, considerably perverted men, rather fractions of a man. *JAF 2.448*

That monstrous tuberosity of Civilised Life, the Capital of England. *Col 1.233* [*Sartor Resartus*]

God's forgiveness to all Cockney "men of wit": they know not what death and Gehenna does lurk in that laborious inanity of theirs: inane speech, the pretence to be saying something when you really are saying *nothing* but only counterfeits of things, is the beginning and basis of all other inanities whatsoever! *CL 15.56* [To John Sterling]

The Bohemians are a different people from the Germans proper. Yesterday not one in a hundred of them could understand a word of German. They are liars, thieves, slatterns, a kind of miserable subter-Irish people — Irish with the addition of ill-nature and a disposition decidedly disobliging. *JAF 4.224*

The whole matter seemed to me to be the very highest flight of Transcendental Cockneyism yet known among mankind. [On Crystal Palace] *JAF 4.153*

Human swinery at its acme. [On Westport workhouse] *JAF 4.5*

"This way to the gents' cabin, sir!" and in truth it was almost worth a little voyage to see such a cabin of gents; for never in all my travels had I seen the like before, nor probably shall again. The little crib of a place which I had glanced at two hours before and found six beds in had now developed itself by hinge-shelves and iron brackets into the practical sleeping-place of at least sixteen of the gent species. There they all lay, my crib the only empty one; a pile of clothes up to the very ceiling, and all round it gent packed on gent, few inches between the nose of one gent and the nape of the other gent's neck; not a particle of air, all orifices closed. Five or six of said gents already raging and snoring, and the smell! Ach Gott! I suppose it must resemble that of the slave-ships in the middle passage. It was positively immoral to think of sleeping in such a receptacle of abominations. *JAF 4.54*

Sunk crown-deep in *Cant*, Twaddle, and hollow Traditionality. [America] *CL 13.208* [To John Sterling]

ON EDUCATION

The other day I went with Murray to call upon Macculloch, the Scotsman. He was sitting like a great Polar bear, chewing, and vainly trying to digest, the doctrines of Adam Smith and Ricardo, which he means to vomit forth again next spring in the shape of lectures to "the thinking public" of this city. *JAF 1.175*

My schoolfellows were boys, mostly rude boys, and obeyed the impulse of rude nature which bids the deer-herd fall upon any stricken hart, the duck-flock to put to death any broken-winged brother or sister, and on all hands the strong tyrannise over the weak. *JAF 1.15*

Better die than be a schoolmaster for one's living. *JAF 1.55*

There is also a schoolmaster right overhead, whose noisy brats give me at times no small annoyance. On a given night of the week he also assembles a select number of vocal performers, whose music, as they charitably name it, is now and then so clamorous that I almost wished the throats of these sweet singers full of molten lead, or any other substance that would stop their braying. *JAF 1.60*

Experience, indeed, will teach him, for Experience is the best of schoolmasters; only the school-fees are heavy. *Col 6.185* ['Goethe's Helena']

I had thought of attempting to become an advocate. It seemed glorious to me for its independency, and I did read some law books, attend Hume's lectures of Scotch law, and converse with and question various dull people of the practical sort. But it and they and the admired lecturing Hume himself appeared to me mere denizens of the kingdom of dullness, pointing towards nothing but money as wages for all that bogpool of disgust. Hume's lectures once done with, I flung the thing away for ever. *JAF 1.64*

I vomited it forth on them like wild Annandale grapeshot. [On his lecture about Mahomet] *JAF 3.181*

Greek words and Latin are fine things, but they cannot hide the emptiness and lowness of many who employ them. *JAF 1.93*

The too well-known product of our method of vocal education — the teacher merely operating on the tongue of the pupil, and teaching him to wag it in a particular way. *Col 11.323* ['Inaugural Address']

Sir, if you have no notion of virtue within your own breast, I despair of ever communicating to you any adequate conception of it. *S 34*

The Hinterschlag Professors knew syntax enough; and of the human soul thus much: that it had a faculty called Memory, and could be acted-on through the muscular integument byappliance of birch-rods. *Col 1.105* [*Sartor Resartus*]

Depend upon it there is a learning more available often than the learning of books, the learning of the ways of men, which cannot be acquired except from conversing with them and observing them. *CL 1.339* [To John A Carlyle]

The grand schoolmaster is Practice. *Col 9.184* [*Corn-Law Rhymes*]

The English Universities and indeed the British are a scandal to this century. *CL 5. 311* [To Macvey Napier]

www.ingramcontent.com/pod-product-compliance
Lightning Source LLC
Chambersburg PA
CBHW072015170626
46813CB00005B/2155